THE LEGENDS OF
KING ARTHUR

MERLIN, MAGIC AND DRAGONS

CB032169

Dados Internacionais de Catalogação na Publicação (CIP) de acordo com ISBD

M469g	Mayhew, Tracey Gawain and the Green Knight / adaptado por Tracey Mayhew. – Jandira : W. Books, 2025. 96 p. ; 12,8cm x 19,8cm. – (The legends of king Arthur)

ISBN: 978-65-5294-166-4

1. Literatura infantojuvenil. 2. Literatura Infantil. 3. Clássicos. 4. Literatura inglesa. 5. Lendas. 6. Folclore. 7. Mágica. 8. Cultura Popular. I. Título. II. Série.

2025-617

CDD 028.5
CDU 82-93

Elaborado por Vagner Rodolfo da Silva - CRB-8/9410
Índice para catálogo sistemático:
1. Literatura infantojuvenil 028.5
2. Literatura infantojuvenil 82-93

The Legends of King Arthur: Merlin, Magic, and Dragons
Text © Sweet Cherry Publishing Limited, 2020
Inside illustrations © Sweet Cherry Publishing Limited, 2020
Cover illustrations © Sweet Cherry Publishing Limited, 2020

Text by Tracey Mayhew
Illustrations by Mike Phillips

© 2025 edition:
Ciranda Cultural Editora e Distribuidora Ltda.

1st edition in 2025
www.cirandacultural.com.br

No part of this publication may be reproduced, stored in a retrieval system, or transmitted in any form or by any means, electronic, mechanical, photocopying, recording, or otherwise, without written permission of the publisher.
This book is a work of fiction. Names, characters, places, and incidents are either the product of the author's imagination or are used fictitiously, and any resemblance to actual persons, living or dead, business establishments, events, or locales is entirely coincidental.

THE LEGENDS OF KING ARTHUR

GAWAIN
AND THE
GREEN KNIGHT

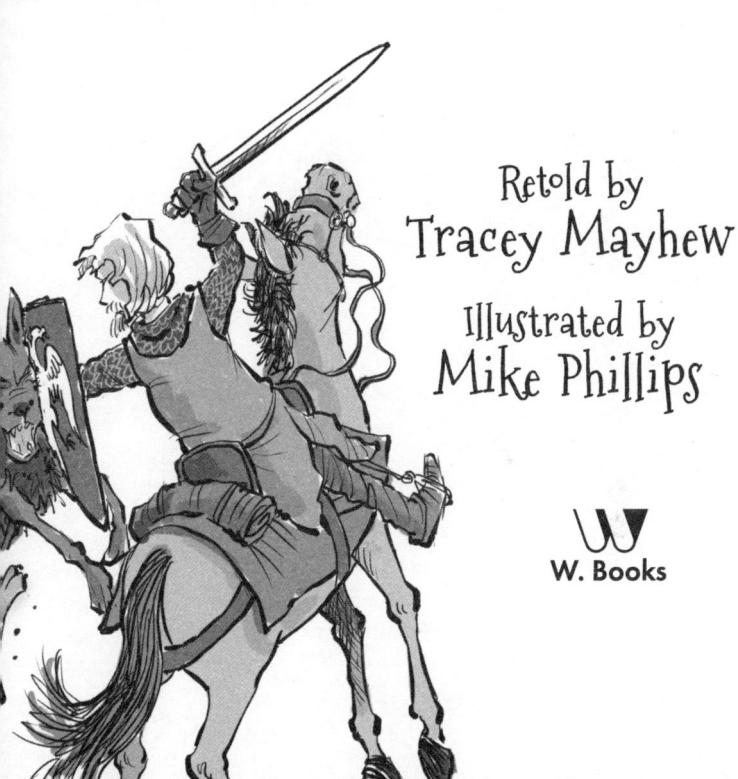

Retold by
Tracey Mayhew

Illustrated by
Mike Phillips

W. Books

Chapter One

Christmas at Camelot was a truly joyous affair. Mistletoe hung in the doorways and holly decorated the tables. It was a time of celebration, filled with laughter and feasts, and good-natured competition amongst King Arthur and his knights.

Every day, Arthur led his men from Camelot to hunt in the neighbouring forests. Each knight hoped that he would be the one to bring back the largest prey, which would become the centrepiece for the feast that evening. But it was for the New Year's feast, the last of the season, that the competition really began.

As the sun rose on New Year's Day, Sir Gawain set out with his fellow knights in high hopes. He had been the most successful in the hunts so far, bringing back over half of the centrepieces. He had no doubt that he would be successful again – until Sir Bedivere brought down a huge boar and was declared the winner.

'It was even bigger than Caball!' Kay declared, as he shared the story in the Great Hall that evening. At the sound of his name, Arthur's largest hunting dog trotted over, hoping for food. Kay laughed, clapping Bedivere on the shoulder. 'Even with only one hand, he's still a better hunter than the rest of us!'

As the laughter rose, Gawain drank his wine in silence, staring at the fire burning brightly in the hearth. Draining his cup, he held it in the air to ask a passing servant to refill it.

'Don't look so dejected!' Kay scolded him. 'Your time will come soon enough.'

'Will it?' Gawain sighed. He had come to Camelot with dreams of greatness. He had been determined to prove himself worthy of his seat at the Round Table, and gain glory for himself and his king. Lately he doubted whether he would ever get the chance.

But Kay was nodding. 'Of course it will! You're young. You have plenty of time to find your quest.'

Gawain glanced up as the king stood abruptly at the front of the room, where he dined with the queen and Merlin.

Guinevere looked particularly lovely in a ruby silk gown and simple gold chain belt.

'Today, we celebrate the New Year!' Arthur announced, looking strong and happy beside her. 'And what better way than with a heroic tale?' The room filled with expectant murmuring as people began looking around, wondering who would speak. 'I wish to hear a tale of bravery and cunning from one of my knights!'

Gawain gripped his cup, wishing he had reason to speak.

Suddenly the main doors burst open with a resounding crash. Icy winter air swept the room, extinguishing dozens of candles in the wrought-iron chandeliers. The shape of a man on horseback filled the doorway.

No. Not a man.

Gawain squeezed his eyes shut in disbelief, but when he opened them again he saw the same thing. Not only was the intruder riding a horse *inside* the castle. Not only was he *enormous*.

He was *green*.

Green all over: from the holly wreath upon his shoulder length green hair, down his armour to his boots. His skin was the colour of a young oak leaf and his beard was the colour of wet moss. Even the blade of the axe hanging at his side looked like it was made of emerald.

The only thing that *wasn't* green were his fiery red eyes that seemed to burn into every soul in Camelot's Great Hall.

Chapter Two

The giant rode a few paces into the room, revealing the slumped bodies of Arthur's guards in the hallway. His fearsome warhorse, which had appeared to be black in the doorway, was now clearly the deepest, darkest green. Its muscles rippled in the candlelight.

'Calm yourselves!' The giant's voice boomed, deep and forceful, as women screamed and men – including Gawain

– scrambled for their weapons. 'I come here for sport, not war!'

'Sport?' Arthur questioned. He spoke calmly enough, but he had maneuvered himself closer to Guinevere. Excalibur glinted at his hip.

The giant dismounted and faced the king. 'Do I stand before Arthur Pendragon?' he asked. Behind him, two of the guards stirred on the floor, dizzily trying to regain their feet. Arthur visibly relaxed when he saw that they had not been permanently harmed.

'You do,' he replied carefully. 'And as king I welcome you to Camelot.' He paused before adding, 'If, as you say, you are not here to fight, perhaps you will join us in our celebrations?'

The giant shook his head. 'I have not come here to eat!'

'Then why have you come?'

'I have heard stories of the bravery and honour of you and your knights. I have come to test the truth of them.'

The hall filled with outraged voices.

'I need one man,' the giant continued. 'One man who will strike me a blow with this axe!' Slipping his axe from his belt, he held the weapon

16

aloft. 'Then, a year from now, I will return the exact same blow.'

The voices fell silent.

A sound like a distant landslide rumbled through the room. The giant was laughing! 'Is this *truly* the court of King Arthur? Are you men *really* the bravest in the land? I think not! You are cowards, I see that now!'

'Give me your axe!'

All heads turned to see Arthur making his way towards the giant.

'I will strike the blow and prove that no one here is a coward.'

The giant handed Arthur his axe, but warned, 'Remember, King of Kings, you have only one blow.'

'One blow is all I need,' Arthur promised as he hefted the axe. It too was huge.

'Wait! Stop, Your Majesty!' Gawain wove his way to where Arthur and the giant stood. 'Let *me* do this,' he pleaded. 'Let me be the one to strike the blow.'

'There's no need,' Arthur insisted.

'Please, uncle. I have been waiting for a chance to prove myself to you and this court. This is it.'

Arthur could not deny such a request. 'So be it,' he agreed.

As Gawain accepted the axe, Arthur leant in close and whispered, 'Aim well and he will not be alive to return the blow next year.'

Gawain nodded his understanding before turning to face the green man.

'My name is Gawain. I accept your challenge.'

'Well, it is good to see that your king has one brave man in his court!' The red eyes glanced disdainfully around the hall. 'Now, Sir Gawain, you must promise, before your king, that you will find me in a year and let me return the blow.'

'Who are you and where will I find you?' Gawain asked. Adrenaline was already coursing through him; along with the certainty that he would never need to know the answer.

'I shall tell you that *after* you have made your blow.'

'As you wish.' Gawain hesitated. 'Would you mind kneeling down?'

The giant laughed again, but dropped readily to his knees. 'There. Is that better?'

The green head was almost level with Gawain's own.

'That's perfect,' Gawain said, and swung the axe.

Chapter Three

The giant did not move, and the axe sliced easily through flesh and bone. The green head fell with a dull, wet thud onto the flagstones, its red eyes staring into the crowd. There was no blood, green or otherwise. Nevertheless …

A triumphant grin spread across Gawain's face. *He'd done it!*

Gawain lifted the axe high and a jubilant cheer filled the hall as hands struck tabletops and cups raised to toast him. King Arthur clapped him on the back.

'A well-aimed blow indeed, nephew! Well done.'

Gawain could hardly believe it. His king was congratulating him, his fellow knights were cheering him – it was all he'd ever wanted.

Then it all stopped.

'Did you see that?' It wasn't clear who spoke. All eyes turned to the headless body of the green giant. Gawain lowered the axe.

'It's moving!' someone else cried.

Gawain frowned. It was impossible! Then he saw it for himself: the green fingers moved. Followed by the arms. The legs.

'Stand back!' Arthur commanded. 'Knights!'

The Knights of the Round Table surged

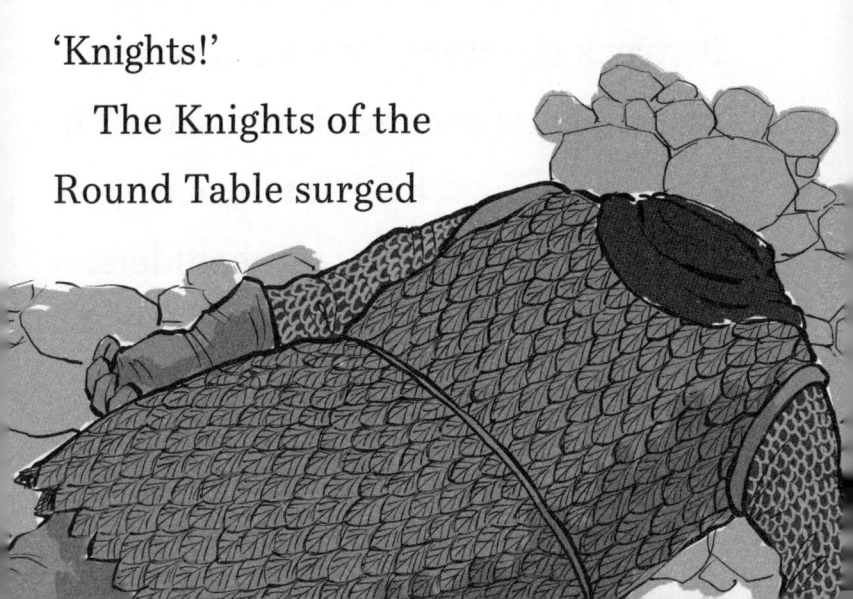

to the front of the crowd, where, to Gawain's horror, the giant's headless body was beginning to sit up.

'What in God's name?' Kay cried, making the sign of the cross over his chest.

The knights drew their weapons. The body's movements were becoming more deliberate, reaching out searchingly and slapping the flagstones with giant palms. Finally it struck the stump of its own neck, picked up its own head, and settled it back into place upon its shoulders.

'Ah, that's better!' the

green man declared, moving his head left and right as if checking the fit.

The intruder was once again blocking the main doors, and the only others in the Great Hall – those leading to the Round Table room – were locked. Instead, panicked guests scrambled to the far end of the hall.

The giant watched them, clearly amused by their fear, but his smile soon faded when he saw the knights with their weapons drawn.

'Surely the brave Knights of the Round Table would not attack an unarmed man?' he mocked.

At these words, the knights looked uncertain, some even lowering their swords.

'What kind of creature are you?' Arthur demanded.

The green man ignored him, focusing only on Gawain.

'You have struck your blow,' he said. 'In a year, you will come find me so that I can strike mine.'

Gawain felt sick. Only a moment ago, he had thought himself so clever!

'Where will you be?' he asked as steadily as he could.

'Ride north from here, through the borderlands,' the giant explained, plucking his axe from Gawain's numb grasp. 'When you think all hope is lost, look to the sky. Follow where your eyes and ears lead you and you will find me, the Green Knight, at the Green Chapel.'

Mounting his horse, the Green Knight made his way unhurriedly back the way he had come. 'One year, Sir Gawain!' he called back. And when the echoes of his voice were gone, when the sound of hooves had faded, Gawain was still staring after him.

Chapter Four

More than once over the months that followed, Gawain regretted speaking up in the Great Hall. But that only made him feel worse. After all, it was far better that *he* should die on such a doomed quest than his king.

Now that time was more precious to him, it passed more quickly. Before Gawain knew it, winter had arrived again, and with it All Saints' Day: the day he was to leave Camelot to find the Green Knight.

King Arthur walked with him to his charger, Gringolet, and Pellinore passed him his shield when he was mounted. Seeing his coat of arms reminded Gawain why he was doing this: he was upholding his knightly code and honouring the promise he had made.

Gawain sat straighter and looked around at the gathered knights. They were sombre and quiet. Everyone knew that he was riding to his death.

'Some farewell this is!' Gawain joked weakly. 'You look as if you took a swig of ale and got a mouthful of water!'

'Some *friend* you are for keeping us out in the cold!' Kay heckled back, his breath misting in the frosty air of the courtyard.

Gawain surprised himself with his first genuine laugh in months. 'Then I will not keep you any longer! A fireplace for you and a quest for me. Farewell!'

A cheer rang out in response, and with a snap of the reins, Gawain and Gringolet set off.

'God speed, Sir Gawain!' Arthur called after him. It was a cry echoed by the rest of the knights.

Out of sight, Gawain's smile fell. From now on, he was on his own.

And he was terrified.

Gawain headed north as instructed. For days, then weeks, he rode through the borderlands. Winter had driven all the animals into hiding, and it was luck more than skill that allowed him to catch the odd hare or bird to roast. Often he had to content himself with whatever berries he could find in the woods, and what little dried meat he had left in his saddlebags.

Cold sapped his strength. And the rain! The sky lashed Gawain for days on end, pounding him until all he could hear was the rain drumming on his armour. It didn't matter how much he tried to clean and dry it by

his campfire each night; at the end of each long day, rust would be setting in again. Gawain feared that parts of it would soon seize up entirely.

The journey was slow and difficult. But through it all, Gringolet trudged

on, his ears almost permanently flicked back as Gawain spoke to him in the absence of anyone else.

Not a day went by that Gawain didn't think about turning back. It was only the promise he had made to the Green Knight and his determination to uphold the knights' code of honour that kept him pushing onwards.

When you think all hope is lost, look to the sky. Follow where your eyes and ears lead you and you will find me.

Gawain had gone over the Green Knight's words repeatedly, but all he saw when he looked to the sky were iron-grey clouds that promised yet more rain. Until one day, during a rare dry spell, Gringolet tensed, slowed his pace, and began to whinny nervously.

'What's the matter, boy?' Gawain asked, patting the horse's neck reassuringly. His eyes searched trees and bushes that had long since lost their leaves. Dim light still made them impenetrable.

Then he heard it: a low growl behind them.

Twisting in the saddle, Gawain

glimpsed a black-grey wolf before it slunk into the shadows on his right. It reappeared from the left. No – this was a second, brown wolf.

Gawain slowly drew his sword, and threaded his other arm through his shield. He was careful not to make any sudden movements.

Another growl drew his attention as a third wolf launched itself at Gringolet, its jaws snapping viciously at his forelegs. Gringolet reared up, kicking wildly. The animal fell to the ground with a thud.

From the corner of his eye, Gawain saw a blur. He brought his shield up just in time to deflect, but the wolf rallied quickly, and was joined by another targeting Gawain's opposite side.

Panicking now, Gringolet danced out of the path of the second wolf, just

as Gawain swept his shield aside, this time deflecting the third, then slashing at it with his sword. It yelped, a bloody gash opening on its flank, before it limped away into the undergrowth.

Squealing now, eyes rolling, Gringolet broke into a gallop. Gawain held tightly on to the reins, glancing back to see if they were being followed. They were. One wolf remained.

His heart pounding, Gawain leant flat across Gringolet's neck, avoiding branches and spurring him on. Gringolet, tired from many days journey, was soon covered in a foam of sweat, his lungs heaving like bellows. More than once he tripped, until Gawain knew that it was just as dangerous to continue as to stop.

Shooting another look back, it appeared that they were alone – but Gawain wasn't fooled. He reined Gringolet to a halt and leapt off,

scanning the trees until the wolf emerged again, snarling and snapping and slinking slowly towards them.

Gawain's grip on his sword tightened, his weight shifting to the balls of his feet …

The wolf leapt.

Faster than his weary mind could track, Gawain was on the ground, his shield trapped between them. He tried

to angle his sword at the wolf's side, but they were grappling too closely. Teeth strained so near his face he felt a spray of drool.

Gawain dropped his sword and fumbled instead for his dagger. Crying out, he drove it into the animal's flank. The wolf shrieked and fell from his shield, giving Gawain time to stagger to his feet. When he had, the wolf was already trailing its bloody hind leg into the undergrowth. The whimpers faded.

Gawain lurched to his horse, so exhausted that his whole body trembled. Gringolet shied away. He was protecting his right foreleg, which gleamed dark and sticky in the gloomy light.

Gawain winced at the deep gash, matted over with cooling blood. It was bad. If it wasn't cleaned properly and stitched soon, Gringolet would be lame or worse. And as for riding him …

Something wet hit Gawain's brow and snaked coldly down his cheek. It was the only warning shot before the grey skies opened again, drenching man and horse in a single breath. Gawain didn't even try to find shelter. It was hopeless.

Overwhelmed, Gawain sank to his knees, face turned up to the rain.

Everything was hopeless.

Tears filled his eyes as desperation filled him. Then, swimming through them, he saw the shadow of a bird circling overhead. A harsh cry split the silence.

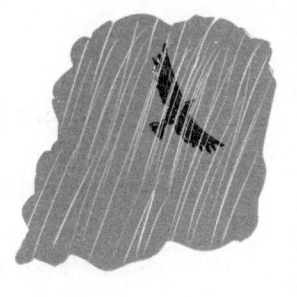

When you think all hope is lost, look to the sky …

Releasing another cry, the hawk hovered directly above him.

Follow where your eyes and ears lead you and you will find me.

It was almost as if it were waiting …

Gawain pushed himself to his feet, his eyes still fixed on the bird as it flew off over the trees. Guiding Gringolet along the path, Gawain followed.

Chapter Five

Gawain made sure he kept the bird in sight. Hope grew in his chest each time he saw it circle back or slow to a hover as if checking on him. The desperation he had felt was fading.

Somehow he knew that the bird would lead him to where he needed to be.

Then they came to a bog.

Standing on the edge of firm ground, Gawain gazed out at pools of black water and swathes of puddled grassland. His heart grew bleak once more. But overhead, the bird's cry rang out.

Gawain shook his head. He had to have faith. He had to believe that on the other side of this bog he would find what he was searching for.

Turning to Gringolet, he said, 'Just one more hardship, boy.'

Half wading, half tottering, Gawain and Gringolet picked their way across the bog. Progress was painstaking.

Gringolet pulled constantly at the reins to go back to dry land, and Gawain often didn't have firm enough footing to resist. Sometimes it felt like for every step forwards he slipped two steps back.

Gawain whispered words of encouragement, splitting his attention between the horse behind him and the bird overhead. Eventually, they reached the trees on the other side. Stepping from their shade, Gawain saw a castle on a bright hillside. It wasn't a chapel, and it wasn't green, but the bird shot towards it and promptly disappeared from view.

'What do you think, boy?' Gawain patted Gringolet. 'Would you like to dry off?

Gawain approached the castle's gatehouse.

'My name is Gawain! I come from Camelot, the court of King Arthur. I seek shelter from your master.'

Taking in the sight of the bedraggled knight, a guard nodded, 'Come, I will take you to him.'

'Thank you,' Gawain said, never more grateful for someone's kindness.

'We will care for your horse, too.'

The guard led Gawain into a courtyard, and signalled for another man to take Gringolet to the stables. Then Gawain was taken to a room where a large man with a red beard sat.

'My lord, Sir Gawain comes from King Arthur's court,' the guard explained.

'You look travel-weary, friend,' the man observed, his voice loud and jovial.

'I am, my lord,' Gawain confessed. 'I come to ask for shelter.'

'Then you shall have it! Never let it be said that Bertilak turns away those in need!'

'Thank you, sir. I assure you, I will only stay until morning. I need to find the Green Chapel by New Year's Day.'

'The Green Chapel is only two miles from here!' Bertilak cried. 'And it is still three days until the New Year. Stay until then and I will send someone to guide you to the chapel myself.'

'You are too kind, my lord.'

Bertilak waved away his thanks. 'Rest now. Tonight you will feast with us.'

The thought of food was too tempting to resist – and Gawain's smile said as much.

'Excellent!' Bertilak beckoned a manservant. 'Go with my man here, Gawain. He will take you to your room and see that a fire is lit, and clean, dry clothes laid out. For now at least, your quest is over.'

Food, warmth, dryness – they were almost enough to make Gawain forget what awaited him at the end of his quest.

Almost.

Later that evening, Gawain made his way to the dining hall, following enticing smells that made his stomach growl.

'Sir Gawain!' cried Bertilak. 'How are you?'

'Much better, sir, thanks to your kindness.' Gone were Gawain's travel-worn clothes, replaced with the fine tunic Bertilak had sent him, and a thickly furred cloak.

'Think nothing of it,' Bertilak replied. 'Come. Let me introduce you to my wife.'

Gawain followed Bertilak through a series of delicious sights and smells. He was so distracted he almost ran into the other man's back when they reached the head table.

'My wife, the Lady Bertilak,' his host announced.

This time Gawain's attention was caught and held fast. Lady Bertilak's beauty surpassed even Guinevere's in his eyes. Her long blonde hair was tied loosely, cascading down her back like molten gold. She wore an ivory dress, trimmed in gold. Beside her sat an old crone, whose dark eyes were sharp and watchful.

'It is an honour to meet you, my lady,' Gawain said, after realising he had been quiet – *stunned* – for some time.

'Sit, Gawain,' Bertilak commanded. 'Let us eat, and hear why you seek the Green Chapel!'

Throughout the meal, Gawain's eyes kept drifting back to Bertilak's wife. Her beauty was captivating and when she smiled at him, he couldn't help returning it, despite her grim companion.

'Since you are so fond of challenges,' Bertilak said at the end of Gawain's story, 'I would like to set you one myself.'

'What kind of challenge?'

'Whatever I hunt in the woods over the next three days, I will give to you, so long as

you give *me* whatever you receive
whilst I am away.'

Gawain nodded easily. 'You have my
word,' he promised.

Chapter Six

Gawain awoke late the following day. Bertilak and his men where already hunting and the castle was quiet. He wandered slowly through the corridors until he found himself once more in the courtyard. From there it didn't take him long to find the stables where Gringolet was resting.

Unlocking the door, Gawain stepped into the stall, patting the horse on the neck. He smiled, pleased to see Gringolet looking more like himself. His wound was neatly stitched.

The horse nuzzled him for a moment before Gawain put his bridle on and led him from the stable. He had no intention of riding him so soon, only to exercise him in the yard.

Outside, Gawain noticed Lady Bertilak watching him from the path and blushed under her gaze. She was still there when he had finished working Gringolet, and returned him to the stall. Her hair shone brightly in the sun and her blue eyes sparkled as she accompanied him back to the castle. The elderly crone was a shadow beside her.

'You look far better today, Sir Gawain, than you did last night,' she observed.

Gawain smiled. 'I have you and your lord to thank for that. I am most grateful for your hospitality.'

'It is our pleasure. Word has spread of your brave deeds.'

Gawain was embarrassed by her words, having lived in fear and dread for months now. 'You honour me with such praise, my lady.'

Her laughter was music to Gawain's ears. 'I honour you with the *truth*, Sir Gawain!' She gave him a kiss on the cheek as they parted, much to Gawain's amazement.

That evening, Bertilak returned to the castle with a deer.

'Sir Gawain, as promised I have hunted this deer in your name,' he announced. 'Do you have anything in return for me?'

The memory of Lady Bertilak's kiss drifted through Gawain's mind and he blushed. 'I do indeed,' he admitted, leaning forwards and kissing his host's cheek.

Bertilak looked confused. 'A kiss? How did you receive such a gift?'

Gawain shook his head. 'The deal was that I would give you whatever I received during my stay, not that I would tell you how I got it.'

Bertilak's laughter echoed around the hall. 'Very true, Gawain! And is that all you received?'

'It is, my lord.'

'Then let us feast!'

The next day, the lady and the crone met Gawain once more, this time as he ate breakfast.

Lady Bertilak approached him, her smile growing as she neared.

'May I ask what you plan to do today, Sir Gawain?' she asked, taking the seat opposite him.

Gawain's eyes shifted to the crone. Her sharp, clear eyes were boring into him.

'I shall see Gringolet again and check on his recovery.'

'He is a fine horse.'

'The finest, my lady.'

Lady Bertilak watched Gawain for a moment before rising. 'Well I wish

you a good day, sir.' Then she leant forwards and kissed both of his cheeks.

That evening, Bertilak returned, this time with a boar. 'This is yours, Gawain,' he declared. 'Now, do you have anything for me?'

Gawain smiled, placing a kiss on each of Bertilak's cheeks.

'Two kisses!' Bertilak exclaimed. 'You have had a lucky day! Is that everything you received?'

Gawain nodded.

'Then let us feast! And maybe you will consider telling me how you came by such wonderful gifts.'

Gawain awoke the next morning to a pounding on his door. Rising, he

dressed quickly, and opened it to find
Lady Bertilak outside. 'My lady!'

'I wish to speak to you, sir!' she
declared, stepping past him into his
chamber.

'What is it? Is something wrong?'

There was fear in her eyes. 'I
am afraid that when you see the
Green Knight tomorrow, you will be
harmed. Must you go?'

'I must keep my word no matter the
consequence.'

'Then take this.' She pressed a
green piece of cloth into his hand.
'This sash has the power to protect
the wearer from harm. Wear it
tomorrow.'

Gawain's glanced down at the cloth, closing his hand slowly around it. 'Thank you, my lady.'

Lady Bertilak kissed him quickly three times on his cheek. 'I should

leave you now. I know you will have much to do before you leave. I shall see you this evening at the feast.'

'Indeed you will, my lady,' Gawain agreed. 'And thank you again.'

When he was alone, Gawain studied the sash.

Could a piece of material protect him tomorrow? He truly hoped so. He did not want to die.

That night Bertilak returned with a fox, and Gawain gave him the three kisses he had received from the lady. When asked if he had received anything else, Gawain shook his head. But hidden beneath his tunic was the green sash.

Chapter Seven

'This is as far I go,' Bertilak's guide announced, looking anxiously at the path to the Green Chapel. Even his horse seemed nervous.

'Thank you for coming this far,' Gawain said.

'The Green Knight is a fearsome enemy, sir. You should turn back–'

'I cannot. I made a promise and
I intend to fulfill it.' Gawain smiled
reassuringly. 'I'll be fine,' he added.
His hand moving to rest over the
hidden green sash wrapped twice
around his torso.

'Then may God be with you,' the guide murmured.

Gawain bowed his head, setting off up the path alone. It wasn't long before it widened onto a grassy clifftop. A hissing sound filled the air: the sound of a whetstone being drawn against a blade.

'You came!' a voice boomed.

Gawain turned to see the Green Knight sitting on a rock, his axe across his lap as he sharpened the emerald blade. His fiery eyes burned.

'Let us end this!' Gawain called, dismounting and coming to stand before him.

The Green Knight stood likewise. 'A year ago, I called you brave,' he said, 'but now I see how true that is. I do not know many men who would travel so far to receive such a blow.'

Gawain thought of all the times he had wanted to turn back during his journey, but held his head high.

'Kneel, Sir Gawain,' the Green Knight instructed. 'As I did for you.'

Gawain knelt.

'And be still,' the Green Knight added. 'As I was before you cut *my* head off.'

Gawain swallowed hard and was still. He waited. And waited. When Gawain finally heard the Green Knight move, he couldn't help it. He flinched.

'You moved,' the Green Knight observed, as his axe missed Gawain's neck by inches. 'Are you afraid, Oh Knight of the Round Table?'

Gawain took a breath, willing himself to be brave. 'I won't move again. Do it.'

Gawain closed his eyes, and waited. This time when he sensed movement, he didn't flinch. He heard the thud of the axe and opened his eyes to find it buried in the grass next to him. 'You missed again!'

The Green Knight laughed. 'But at least you didn't flinch again!'

Gawain frowned, annoyed. 'Get it over with!' he growled.

'As you wish.'

The axe lifted a third and final time, as Gawain bowed his head once more. This time, as it fell, Gawain felt a quick, searing pain. In a panic, he covered his neck with his hand. But it was only a scratch. Blood barely trickled through his fingers. He was still very much alive.

Leaping to his feet, Gawain drew his sword. 'One blow, you said. Well, you've had your blow and now I can fight you!'

The Green Knight's laughter rang through the clearing. 'Calm down, Gawain. This was all a test. A test you have passed.'

Gawain watched, stunned, as a
green mist rose up and engulfed his
opponent. When it faded,
he found himself
facing ... '*You!*'

Bertilak smiled. 'I hope you can forgive me, Gawain.'

'But ... I don't understand.'

'You were always meant to find your way to my castle; that was where you were tested. You see, for the first two days of your stay, you were honest. You told me about the kisses you received, and for that honesty I deliberately missed your neck twice with my axe. But on the third day, you lied.'

Gawain bowed his head in shame.

'You never told me about the sash you wear,' Bertilak reproached him, 'and for that I gave you a glancing blow.'

'I *was* afraid,' Gawain admitted. 'Fear made me flinch, and fear made me lie. How can I have passed your test?'

'Being fearless and being brave are not the same thing. You cannot be brave if you have no fear. But to be afraid and yet act in spite of it, as you have done: *that* is brave. You are a worthy knight, Sir Gawain, and I believe that you have learnt your lesson about honesty.'

'Nevertheless,' Gawain vowed, pulling the green fabric from under his armour, 'from this day forwards, I shall wear this sash. To remind myself to always be honest, even in the face of fear.'

Bertilak nodded approvingly.

'Then it is finished?' Gawain asked. 'The challenge is over?'

'*Our* challenge is over,' Bertilak replied, 'but there is another who seeks to challenge all of Camelot.'

'Who?'

'Morgan le Fay. The old crone you met at my castle. It is she who was behind all of this. It is she who sent me to Camelot. She wants nothing more than to create trouble for King Arthur.'

'Then I must return and warn him,' Gawain exclaimed, sheathing his sword.

Saying goodbye to Bertilak, Gawain began his long journey back to Camelot, where everyone was just as shocked to see him as they were delighted. After warning them of Morgan le Fay's dark intentions, it was with some reluctance that Gawain told them of his adventures, for he was

still ashamed of his weakness in lying. But neither his king nor his fellow knights blamed him. And since the same weakness ran in all of them, each also decided to wear a green sash as a reminder to always be honest.

CONTINUE THE QUEST WITH THE NEXT BOOK IN THE SERIES!

"This series opens the door to a treasure house of wonderful stories which have previously been available chiefly to older readers. We can only welcome it as a fabulous resource for all who love magical tales, and those who will come to love them."

JOHN MATTHEWS

AUTHOR OF THE RED DRAGON RISING SERIES AND ARTHUR OF ALBION